FAVOURITE CLASSICS
TREASURE ISLAND

Retold by Sasha Morton
Illustrated by Alfredo Belli

Ticktock

An Hachette UK Company
www.hachette.co.uk

First published in Great Britain in 2013 by Ticktock,
an imprint of Octopus Publishing Group Ltd
Carmelite House
50 Victoria Embankment
London, EC4Y 0DZ
www.octopusbooks.co.uk
www.ticktockbooks.co.uk

ISBN 978 1 78325 269 5

A CIP record for this book is available from the British Library.

Printed and bound in China

10 9 8 7 6 5 4 3 2 1

Series Editor: Lucy Cuthew Design: Advocate Art
Managing Editor: Karen Rigden
Senior Production Manager: Peter Hunt

Contents

The Characters

Jim Hawkins

Long John Silver

Billy Bones

Black Dog

Pew

Dr Livesey

Squire Trelawney

Captain Smollet

Ben Gunn

Chapter 1
A Mysterious Guest

It was some years ago now, but the day I met Billy Bones was the day my life changed forever.

My name is Jim Hawkins. My mother owns an inn called The Admiral Benbow, on the south-west coast of England. Billy Bones came out of the mist one morning with his belongings in a wooden seaman's chest and a white scar across one cheek.

The Admiral Benbow

"Do you get many visitors here?" he asked.

My mother shook her head.

"Then this is the place for me," he declared.

Billy spent his days looking out to sea with his spyglass. Every evening, he would ask if any seafaring men had come by. We learned these were the type of men he was trying to avoid.

By night, Billy sat by the fire in the bar, telling tales of his adventures on the high seas to anyone who would listen, and singing old sea-songs.

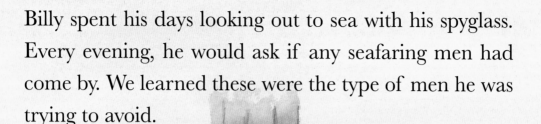

"Fifteen men on the dead man's chest! Yo, ho, ho, and a bottle of rum!"

he would sing.

Billy offered me a silver four-penny every month if I would look out for

'a terrifying-looking, seafaring man with one leg'

for him.

How that man haunted my dreams! On stormy nights when the wind howled around our house I would lie awake, and imagine him coming for me.

One frosty January morning, another strange man startled me.

"Is this where my old mate Billy is staying?"

he asked, in a menacing voice. Although he
had both legs, I noticed that one hand was
missing two fingers and that he had a cutlass
under his coat.

I told the man that Billy was out, but to my dismay, he hung around the inn to wait for him. Before long, Billy strode towards the pub. The stranger stepped out and Billy gasped,

"Black Dog!"

"That's right. Black Dog has come to see his old shipmate Billy Bones," the man cackled.

I could hear a low murmuring from Black Dog and cries of "No, no!" from Billy. All of a sudden, Black Dog fled the inn and I found Billy collapsed on the ground, groaning, "I must leave here!"

Chapter 2
The Black Spot

"The doctor said I have to stay in bed for a week, Jim. I can't! They'll have the black spot on me by then," fretted Billy.

It turned out that Billy, Black Dog and the man with one leg who Billy feared, had been crewmates on a pirate ship owned by Captain Flint. When Flint died, he gave Billy a map that showed where he had buried all of his stolen treasure. Putting the 'black spot' on him would mean Billy would have to meet with Flint's old crew and hand over the map… **or face death.**

The next morning, out of the mist came a strange tapping noise and the most fearsome-looking man I have ever seen appeared next to me. He twisted back my arm and hissed in my ear,

"Take me to Billy Bones or I'll break your arm."

I did as he demanded with shaking legs and a pounding heart.

Billy looked up at the man and gasped,  **"Pew!"** Pew put a note in Billy's palm and said grimly,

"Now it is done."

The man ran out of the inn and Billy opened his hand to show me the 'black spot'. Then, without any warning, Billy dropped dead.

YOU HAVE UNTIL TEN TONIGHT

I found my mother and explained what had just happened.

Even with Billy dead, the men would still be coming for him and whatever he was hiding!

I found the key to Billy's sea-chest around his cold, dead neck. At the very bottom of the chest lay a bundle, tied up in oilcloth that I shoved into my pocket. Just then, we heard the same tapping that had signalled Pew's arrival before. And we heard shouting from the nearby hill as well. Captain Flint's men were on their way and the inn was no longer safe for us to stay in.

We leapt from a window and ran, hidden by the thick sea mist, to hide under a nearby bridge. But before long, the mist began clearing!
The moonlight would soon expose us to the men.

We could hear three pirates shouting to each other as they stormed inside the pub.

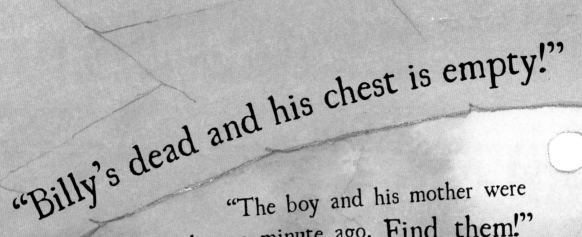

"Billy's dead and his chest is empty!"

"The boy and his mother were here a minute ago. **Find them!**"

The men's footsteps started to clatter up the road, getting ever closer to us. Just then, we saw a group of riders galloping towards the inn. The men scattered, but Pew was trampled by the hooves of one of the horses. I opened the bundle from Billy's sea-chest, and was astounded to find that it held a treasure map.

Chapter 3
Treasure Island

I could think of only one person who would know what to do with the map and so I rode hard all the way to the Squire's mansion in the village. Our family doctor, Livesey, who was a good man, happened to be visiting. The three of us spread Billy's treasure map out on the table before us.

"I will have this treasure found within the year!" decided Squire Trelawney. "I will put together a crew and prepare the best ship in England. Livesey, you will be the ship's doctor and young Jim here will be the cabin boy."

"What's written there?" I asked, noticing something scrawled on the back of the map.

Tall tree, Spy-glass shoulder, N.N.E.
Skeleton Island, E.S.E. Ten feet.
Seven hundred thousand pounds.

We each were sworn to secrecy. No-one must know the real reason for our voyage. After all, the pirates who had ransacked the inn were still looking for Captain Flint's map and treasure. Within three weeks, Dr Livesey and I were summoned to Bristol Docks.

I said a fond farewell to my mother and set off on my big adventure.

The docks
themselves
were like a new
world to me and my
desire to be at sea grew
by the minute! Ships of
all sizes bobbed on the water
as sailors climbed their rigging
high above my head. Somewhere
in the middle of all of the activity was
our ship, and tomorrow we would set sail!

In the morning, the Squire sent me to the Spy-glass Tavern. Its owner, Long John Silver, was to be ship's cook. He had even helped the Squire to gather together the ship's crew.

Long John Silver hopped across the room swinging a crutch where his left leg should have been. Surely he couldn't be Billy Bones's feared one-legged man? No! This man was far too decent. Then, I saw Black Dog, the man who had betrayed Billy Bones! He saw me and suddenly fled.

"That man was in my house – he is a criminal!" I cried. "Stop him!"

"And now he's leaving my house without paying his bill!" shouted Silver.

He questioned me over how I knew such a dishonest fellow and by the time Silver's men returned empty-handed, I was convinced that Silver was a good man, who had never met Black Dog before. How wrong I was.

Together, we set off
for our ship,
The Hispaniola.

At last we were ready to set sail, but our Captain, a man called Smollett, was not happy.

"I have learnt we are going after treasure, with a crew that I've never met before. And all of them know that we are to hunt treasure, before I do myself. Something about this is not right!" he declared.

What Captain Smollett feared most of all was a mutiny at sea.

Could we trust this crew?

Despite the Captain's misgivings, the anchor soon came up.

Long John Silver cried,
"Fifteen men on the dead man's chest!"
and the crew roared back,
"Yo, ho, ho, and
a bottle of rum!"

We were on our way to Treasure Island!

Chapter 4
Mutiny!

Our outward voyage went well. Long John Silver kept us well fed and by coincidence, owned a parrot named Captain Flint after the infamous pirate whose treasure we were seeking.

"Pieces of eight! Pieces of eight!" the parrot squawked constantly.

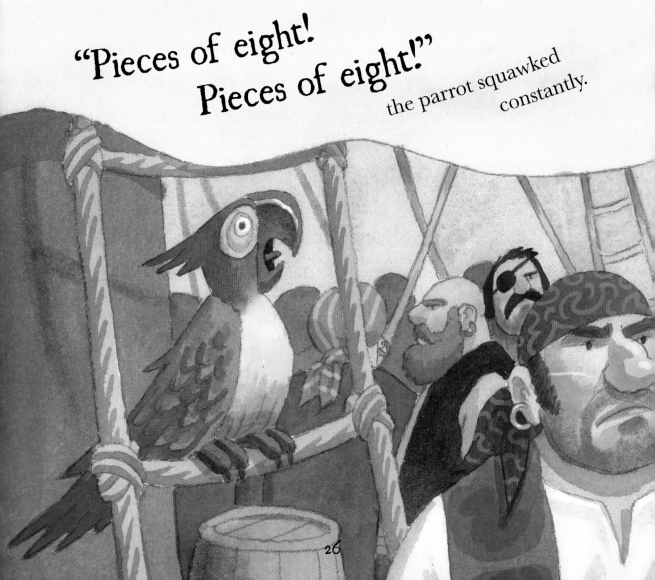

But on the last day at sea, I overheard talk that proved the suspicions of Captain Smollett.

I had hopped into the fruit barrel to find one of the last apples in it and whilst inside, I overheard Long John Silver and some of his old crewmates plotting together. There was indeed a mutiny afoot!

"As you know, most of us aboard are Flint's old crew. A share of his treasure is no more than we deserve. We'll load up the treasure, then leave those that aren't on our side on the island and sail away as rich men," said Silver, pleased with his cunning plan.

"Land Ho!" they cried as the island came into view.

I quickly found the Captain and told him every detail of Long John Silver's plan.

We decided to land and continue to seek the treasure, whilst keeping an eye on Silver and his men. If we confronted them now, there might be fighting, and we were too few to take them on. On the deck, the Captain made an announcement.

"My lads, a turn ashore will hurt nobody. I'll fire a gun before sundown to signal you back aboard."

Everyone began to climb into the boats. In a flash, I jumped aboard one of the rowing boats too, but soon began to regret what I had done. I was alone with men I now knew to be pirates!

As the boat neared some shoreside trees, I grabbed an overhead branch and swung myself out to get away from them.

"Oi! Jim! Get him! Jim!" I heard Silver shout menacingly. I ran into the undergrowth as fast as I could.

I was so relieved to have given Silver the slip, that I enjoyed exploring the island until a tall figure leapt towards me from behind a tree.

"Who are you?"
I asked, terrified.

He croaked:
"I am Ben Gunn.
I was marooned
on this island by
Long John Silver and Billy Bones.
But I'll tell you a secret, boy. I'm rich!"

I doubted that very much, but I managed
to explain that Long John Silver
was in charge of a mutiny
and that trouble was
about to begin.

"I built a boat and hid
it behind the white rock,"
Gunn babbled.

Suddenly, we heard the thunderous noise of the cannon!

"They have begun to fight!" I shouted. Together we
ran for the beach until we saw the Union Flag fluttering in the
air from a wooden fort before us.

As soon as Ben Gunn saw the flag, he said, "That must be your friends, hiding out in Flint's old wooden stockade."

We could see The Hispaniola in the bay, with the pirate's flag flying from her mast. Ben left me to keep an eye on our enemies, while I found my old friends and three other members of the crew inside the small fort.

As night fell, Silver approached waving a white flag of truce. "In return for the treasure map," said Silver, "you have my word that all of you will live."

"We do **not** accept your offer," declared Captain Smollett.

"Then we'll be back," threatened Silver, "and them that die will be the lucky ones."

Indeed, Silver's attack on the stockade began soon after. We heard the cackle of his parrot, cawing **"Pieces of eight!"** as his men approached. Somehow, we held our ground and after what seemed like hours, the pirates finally melted into the night.

Chapter 5
The Return of Jim Hawkins

That night, I crept from the safety of the stockade and scrambled along the beach. I planned to cut The Hispaniola adrift, to prevent the pirates from sailing off with the treasure. Soon, I found the white rock that Ben Gunn had described and hidden behind it was his boat!

The tide was in my favour, and soon I drew alongside the ship. Clutching hold of the anchor cable, I cut through one strand after another. Just as the final strand went slack, I grabbed the end of the rope and shimmied up it until, with a final heave, I *toppled* head-first onto the deck.

I sailed the ship, as best as a boy could, back towards the island. As the sun rose, I saw a remote cove that was the perfect place to hide the ship. Alas, just then, a pirate sentry awoke.

**"Why? Who?
What do you think
you're doing, lad?"**
he shouted.

I quickly climbed up the rigging, out of his reach, just as the heavy wooden boom swung around and knocked the pirate flying overboard, never to be seen again. The ship was beached, but thankfully hidden. I waited until darkness before setting back off to the stockade.

A fire was burning outside the building and I started to sense danger. Just then a shrill voice broke the silence around me and struck fear into my heart like a dagger!

"Pieces of eight!
Pieces of eight!"

I turned and ran headlong into Long John Silver himself! Not only had the pirates overpowered my friends and turned them out of the stockade, Silver now had the treasure map in his possession. Despite having no way to leave the island, Silver's mutineers were still anxious to find the treasure!

The next day, Dr Livesey found me tied up
outside the stockade.

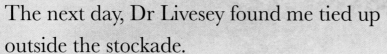

"I ran away from here to save the ship!"
I whispered to him. "She is beached in the North Inlet."

Dr Livesey nodded silently before
he quickly turned and disappeared into the forest.

Soon, the pirates set off with the map towards Spy-glass Hill. There was a rope tied around my waist so I could be led by Silver. I could clearly recall the directions to the treasure:

Tall tree, Spy-glass shoulder, N.N.E. Skeleton Island, E.S.E. Ten feet.

It took time to locate one tall tree in a whole forest and soon Silver's men grew irritable. They became extremely unnerved by the horrible discovery of a skeleton pointing its bony arm in the direction that we were heading.

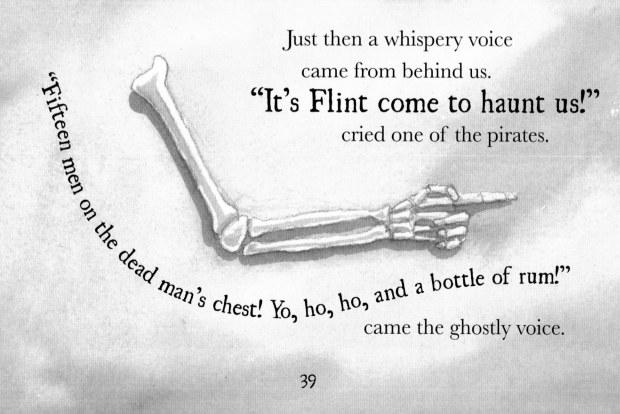

Just then a whispery voice came from behind us.

"It's Flint come to haunt us!"

cried one of the pirates.

"Fifteen men on the dead man's chest! Yo, ho, ho, and a bottle of rum!"

came the ghostly voice.

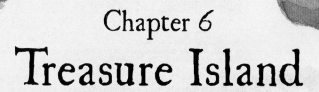

Chapter 6
Treasure Island

"**S**omeone is trying to make fools of us," shouted Silver. "I'm off to dig up Flint's gold."

Dragging me along with him, we raced forwards when Silver stopped abruptly. Before us lay a hole and within it lay a single silver coin.

Someone had beaten us to it. **The treasure was gone!**

Long John Silver's face went white.

"Jim," he whispered, "stand by for trouble."

Leaping

into the empty pit, the rest of the pirates dug with their bare hands to find any gold coins.

Ben Gunn and Dr Livesey rushed up to us and captured Silver. They cut me free and led us to Ben's secret cave, leaving the pirates to their frantic digging.

Knowing how superstitious Flint's pirates were about ghosts, Ben had had the clever idea of singing the crew's song to scare them. Now they were trapped on a haunted island **without any gold to enjoy!**

In his three years of wandering the island, Ben Gunn had discovered Captain Flint's treasure and moved it here! Inside his cave I could see great heaps of coins and bars of gold that stretched far into the shadows.

By the time Silver got the map, it was worthless.

Over the next few days, we loaded the treasure aboard The Hispaniola. It was agreed that the fortune was to be divided between Squire Trelawney and all of his brave men, including myself and the heroic Ben Gunn.

Silver would be taken back to England to stand trial for mutiny.

We decided to maroon the remaining pirates on the island and left them a good stock of supplies before we set sail. As we rounded the island, we saw them pleading to be taken back with us, but we could not risk another mutiny.

Finally, we had left Treasure Island behind.

The journey back was hard and we stopped in Southern America to hire extra hands. But one evening, we discovered Long John Silver had escaped.

He was desperate to avoid being tried for mutiny, so had stolen a rowboat and fled with a bag holding three or four hundred guineas. Despite being frustrated at losing the pirate who had nearly been the end of us, we were all rather pleased to be rid of Silver so cheaply!

These adventures happened many years ago, and we all lived happy lives as wealthy men. I still wonder what might have happened to Long John Silver, but even now, as a grown man, nothing would make me return to that island. For night after night, in my darkest dreams, I still hear the words that make my blood run cold…

"Pieces of eight!"